Stories have always been medicine. And what is medicine but a movement toward the center? Written in a precise voice with exacting language, *Planked bys the Abyss*, is a descent and a reckoning. Sometimes a yawp, sometimes a punch, but always a movement toward the things that must be said and can only be said by this writer. Simply stunning.

—Dominique Christina, Author, Educator, and Conceptual Installation Artist

Meg Tuite's towering imagery is premium poetic; it sparks and catapults the thought of each sentence beyond the center then pulls everything right back to the core. Pay close attention! Intentional outlying signals stitch their properties onto each narrative's promise. Lines like "She leaned into the hours of a clock," "Don't get all drizzly on me now. I got lightning beating thunder under this skin," and, "Damn if she isn't vertical as a dead marriage," remind me of how good it is to have surrealist escape hatches tucked away in a hurtling life. *Planked By the Abyss* is a taut and sharply-awakening collection that goes to the top of my go-to reading pile when I need a shot of creative caffeine. I'm a huge fan of Meg Tuite's writing, and you should be too.

—Ignatius Valentine Aloysius, author of the novel, *Fishhead*. Curator and host of the popular reading series Sunday Salon Chicago

Meg Tuite's new collection brims with voluptuous sentences and deep emotion. Whether they are flash fictions or narrative poems, about Robert Crumb's brother or an unnamed dying woman in hospice, they are all love and pain, humor and profound sadness. Tuite's work is alive with wonder, always asking, how is that we make it through this life? She has no answer but shows us the way nonetheless. Tuite is the master of this short hybrid form, shying away from nothing, opening up the reader's heart with her stunning words.

—**Paula Bomer, author of *Inside Madeline***

In Meg Tuite's exquisite and clever collection, *Planked by the Abyss*, each compressed and swelling line scars the tragic with hope and burns triumphantly. Page by page dense and willowy prose grabs the reader by the throat while ticking humor slices with titles like, "Runaway pronoun for grief," "It's never lonely in a leotard," and "Every kid knows the price." Storm full legged with Tuite through these domestic spaces of marriages, moves, deaths, drinks, drives, and oh, the bodies of broken and brave children. You'll find the rough rub and rush of tattered life all here in lines pulled mesmerizingly taut and slack as marionettes.

—**Deirdre Fagan, author of *Phantom Limbs*
and *Find a Place for Me***

Meg Tuite's *Planked by the Abyss* is a soiled jubilation of hacked adenoids, pithy dimples, road trips, a prescient elephant, and a horny chihuahua. With fearless juxtapositions and raging rhyme, Tuite guides us through a world that conjures destruction while demanding awe. It is a place of artistic salvation and wonder, even as death looms, reminding us how marvelous and doomed we are.

—**Wendy Oleson, author of *Everywhere, Tony Danza***

No one writes sentences like Meg Tuite, who has a voice so unique it's a literary fingerprint. These stories are alive and unpredictable, beautiful and dangerous like a forest of angel's trumpets. With unmistakable style, Tuite captivates in sentences so oddly poetic, so deeply surreal, they are sentient beings blooming with bizarro brilliance and the bewitchingly, timely wisdom of uncanny reality.

—**Aimee Parkison, author of** *Suburban Death Project*

We might have to make up a new category of flash fiction for what Meg Tuite does. Reading *Planked by the Abyss* is not only like reading something completely different, but like reading for the first time. Each of Tuite's sentences feel like a poem. Put together into a story, they feel like an experience. Put together all the stories and it's like I have a new perspective I could never have foreseen, a new understanding of what fiction can do.

—**Michael Czyzniejewski, author of**
The Amnesiac in the Maze: Stories

PLANKED BY THE ABYSS

PLANKED BY THE ABYSS

ISBN 978-1-952600-52-4

First Whiskey Tit Paperback Edition

Book design by Adam Robinson. Cover collage by Kevin Sampsell.

Published in the United States by Whisk(e)y Tit:
WWW.WHISKEYTIT.COM
WWW.MEGTUITE.COM

If you wish to use or reproduce all or part of this book for any means, please let the author and publisher know. You're pretty much required to, legally.

Planked by the Abyss

Meg Tuite

WHISK(E)Y TIT PRESS
Hancock, Vermont

INSIDES

The Shuffle In Your Stare

L et this rummage of uterine captivity undress itself until years of a life unchord my spine, rot the teeth, and styrofoam the skin. Alcohol recognizes me. Drugs are just closer cousins. Basement vantage breaks open gray through the bruised pane in a neighborhood in a city. Blurred tattoos, hairspray, and leakage of brute rage blister some kind of forward movement. Anyone watch the act of change scare itself? I'm fluent in gaping cracks poling me with swelling innards and transient bleeds.

No, I did recognize time grit my tailspin in a sick embrace. It sustains me. The dead flower collection is a preamble to beauty's naked leer of misery. Doesn't everyone simmer daylight until it evaporates, wait for the burner of yellow sky to swelter the inner thighs? Sticky and half-baked hope of what becomes just another pock-marked skeleton drunk on its own marrow.

Speaking From the Tomb

The hollow monotony vibrates through porous mouths. Intoxication of sky lodges its devouring yawn between humans and me. Cigarettes blind the muttering gestures of chronic language. Overdressed meals and hearsay crumble their butts in the ashtray. I flaunt idle. Eyes vast and explosive as Ukraine.

Raging internal desire emanates from Mother's wheelchair on the balcony. Particles of her are unable to spark synapses of flames she used to implode. Power basks in solitude. Can a story parch a death? Mother is bathed in spellbound pallor of promise. Detonate her with stories, plays, endings obese with resurrection.

Mother dies. I shut-up. A pain of shriveled control affronts and tags me as a charlatan. Who believes in my spindled prose? Childhood is huge and envelopes even the most passive semen from extended brethren. 'Fresh flesh' they pin me. Haughty cousins, uncles raw with the junk of their sewage take me as their inheritance.

Vague reality is rudderless past lives. My power lies in lack of memories and visions.

"You shall know the truth and the truth shall make you odd."

~ FLANNERY O'CONNOR

She Got The Her On Him Who They Still Speak Of In Relapsed Gender

News gunned across every church from Springfield to Mississippi after the birth of Abigail. Her mother, Nancy's womb belted the length of the Union States. When her water broke, she drained more than 3,000 square miles through central Illinois and flash flood corn and pumpkin seeds her father had planted. When Nancy farted, she could manage a perfect C and A-minor chord depending on the time of day. Some say the infant was longer than a train traveling through 180 cities and seven states. Others said the Sangamon river hissed and spectacled over 264 miles to the Illinois River. Size was the least of Nancy's worries. Shortly after the birth, objects started nose-diving out of her vagina. Several empty bottles of Brandy, most of someone's cattle, a dozen cats, a few pigs, a horse, turkey, goat, and more than a crate-full of Bibles.

When Nancy's melancholy descended on Abby, the littlest busk of three children, Nancy was listless, trembling, and a stench bayed over her breath of cattle, sheep, and horses. The doctor said it was Milk Sickness after they tried to get her out of bed. When she vomited without stop and an odor of chemicals presumed off the skin, the doctor prepared the family for the worst.

Thomas, the imperious, fuddled father of this tribe was a farmer, a carpenter, but couldn't read or write. He was forthright in his rage, humiliated any scribbled page that dared question him. He sequestered another wife, Sarah, who lived three cabins over, a few weeks after Nancy shriveled.

Abby grew up in the countryside eating five meals a day beneath legs surging upwards toward new horizons, over mountains, long faces, furies, evasions; she grew and grew and once again, grew. Never cared that a suitor could find her, she bent over rooms to enter them. The younger brother died. The sister had notches in the wood of the door frame. Thomas, their father, threw his knife up into the wood beams. That's as near as Abby would ever come to a measurement.

Abby's second mother, Sarah, came with a pack of children. She took a liking to Abby whose clothes were stitched for midgets and kept Abby from standing straight for years. Sarah put her needlework aside and started sewing clothes out of women's quilts and scraps from clucking pouches of Kentucky tongues. Sarah found the perfect log and set it along Abby's back and between her armpits. Abby rose into the sky, one of the first true phoenix' of the 1800's.

And so why, the subterfuge of gender? Abby racked through the headwinds of jobs available for females? Domestic servant, farm worker, tailor and washerwoman. Son of no gun, she said. I'm planting oak tree feet in the god damned white house. I am to be a president.

News swam its way to the Carolinas where Andrea Andrew Johnson waited her turn.

After that, it became hersay:

Ulalia Ulysses Grant
Ruth Rutherford Hayes   Janey James Garfield

Memories That Smell Like Mother

Henry's diary was a soiled jubilation of a recluse's child-hood, stuffed under his iguana's terrarium, that reeked of fierce terror and hands-on scrutiny of grade school intimacy and psychopathy, page by flourished page, inflamed bedlam of erect body odors as purposeful and gusty as the sticky names recorded and blacklisted in backwash gray marker mapping who slithered under-soaped flesh out of station wagons into over-sparkled classrooms cloned with crappy kid's art and Mom bumper stickers flush with joy, love, and clasped community hands, the cloakroom hooked with Henry through Thursday's lunch, pizza day, by Fat Johnson who taunted Henry when he wore Mom's plaid-poly pants suits and told the class he was a designer just like on TV, and then the blacked out days when only a black marker would do after weekends at the lake, Henry's globular face stung by teeming multitudes of mosquitos when Mom knew he was brutally allergic, even when one of the Monday's, after their getaway, was school photo day and Henry had to plaster his face with creamy slabs of beige cover-up Mom kept in her stash for those years with Dad, and reoccurring thoughts of offing himself after adolescent evening breast-feedings to Hank Williams tunes that kept Henry's insomnia potent, his writing crooning across each unsung page, and the early stages of lactose intolerance alive and burgeoning when he gagged in the cafeteria over lukewarm milk cartons slapped on to each tray.

Who Left Mom Alone?

Faceless Mom drapes quilts towels sheets fat-coated with dead animals and family thick against windows. Windows purse lips and press their sweaty hot cheekbones high against panes of push-pinned fabrics. Fabrics haughty with density of weave cross their legs and shout 'fuck off' to anyone searching for a peep. Peep not into her delicate eldest son, Charles anonymous brilliance who writes backwards and upside down, a brush with gauzy histories of windowless, candled rooms worthy of protection. Protection would give his life for Faceless Mom in the dark and wants to permeate her silent screams to be left alone inside his muted mouth. Mouth full of marbles, Charles forges out once a week for groceries, cigarettes, and pencils with his eyes tracing sidewalk cracks, exactly 444 to the corner market.

Marketeer, Robert, is the famous younger son of Mom who needs cash. Cash needs to revisit his past rant with fame. Fame grants a camera team to implode in on the fortress of the two family members Robert financially supports and then hacks. Hacked without warning, Faceless Mom and Charles hear assault outside their apartment stomp, blather, laugh. Laughing as Robert unlocks the front door, beckons the rowdy posse in with a wave. Wave like a sparrow formation encompasses, encroaches their space. Space has become a frigid gust of feral from Mom and Charles. Charles drops his head and pulls up his pants, blocks himself with fists that team up with his cloudy eyes. Eyes stranded with thoughts unable to pretend to connect with outside predators. Predators are humans who eye the fault lines in others, corner it, reign it in. In comes Robert, the famous son, squalling on about how lunacy has a tight noose on their family. Family is his latest spread. Spread the word. Word is a documentary titled 'Crumb'. Crumbs are crazy. Crazy Mom attempts to talk to a camera with the shaky vocals of a prisoner.

Imprison is a word which agoraphobics understand. Understand that when you cross that threshold, you parody a place that is sacred. Sacred is the pink scar that keeps bleeding from your ego.

～～～

Charles, who Robert Crumb acknowledges as his main artistic influence, no longer draws, has never lived on his own, and took prescriptions to help stabilize his mental state (he committed suicide before the film was released).

Whoever Asked a Seashell
How Old It Was?

U pholstered and isolated, food is canned and repressed, but beverages corner the caged scars of summer. I suck the marrow out of bottles. Today the kid has friends over, ravenous for anything. All pithy dimples, luster and mutiny, they're a line-up of grenades on the couch. Wish there was a beta-blocker between me and them, but the goddamn medicine cabinet is gaping dusty rings around the thirty-day supply's that used to showcase there. Expired insurance crumbles time into missed appointments that smirk.

Walmart shopped me yesterday and bless the vodka in bulk that ended up in my bag. I crank shots in the pantry. "How's your mom, dad", I rat-a-tat-tat without recognition of who is who. Four boys launch into *can we just slam the door on this bullshit*, singing, "Good," "Good," "Good," "Good," as I stare through the tangled fidgetry of their captivity. They wait for me to bludgeon them with parental bleating. Jacked-up teenagers hounded by adults who don't give a shit about them is mirrored in their demeanor. Not only am I not that brand of parent, but bullet swigs deepen a need to plumb the surly taste of any boy who finds himself stranger to his body.

The bloated intruder and dewy ingenue of myself paints potency of malleable flesh into a softer shade of a telescope gone wrong side up. The more I drink, the faster calendars unhinge from their years. Blossoms fluent in Spring magnify and hone in on my ripening cheeks.

"You boys want some beer?"

"People dread silence because it is transparent; like clear water, which reveals every obstacle—the used, the dead, the drowned, silence reveals the cast-off words and thoughts dropped in to obscure its clear stream. And when people stare too close to silence they sometimes face their own reflections, their magnified shadows in the depths, and that frightens them. I know; I know."

~Janet Frame

Hospice Care Suffers No Down Time

Clouds rake across the sky, my pancreas. A Chinese doctor says my pulse is dry, white. An exact description of the only wine I buy and suck down every night. I stick out my tongue. He nods and writes down notes I don't care to decipher. He loads up a bag with tonics the color of dead leaves.

Everyone is dying in my daily life. I sit with a woman when an emerald green liquid starts to foam up from the depths of her. Her daughter and I put a flashlight down her throat and see it is thick and moving like lava up, up, up. We are captivated while her husband paces and roars in the background "WE TREAT OUR PETS BETTER THAN THIS." His wife has been actively dying for weeks. She hasn't eaten. Her mouth plies open as I drip water and morphine into it. Every night is the last night. The daughter and I say goodbyes. Every morning she breathes and rasps, mammoth teeth exposed.

The strength and girth of those incisors alone might keep her bound to this planet.

And, one day, as absurd as horror of routine, she dies. I lose a friend, another family, and a job.

And the clouds? Those warriors compliment sleep here in the desert where the sun stalks over 300 days a year. I am tired. The phone still rings. A number flashes across my screen from the house where the woman just died. Obliged to pick up, the familiar voices plead.

Turns out the husband wanted to die. His neighbors heard a gunshot at three in the morning and called the cops. He missed his heart by inches.

The chaplain asks if I can return, take care of him and his wound. Yes. It's an easy transition. I know the terrain. But now, he's not yelling.

He says, "I had a chance, and fucked it up."

I listen and work on cleaning and bandaging his wound. He wants to see my clouds.

"Maybe I should have called a vet," he says.

"Vets are more expensive," I say.

Flee With Hank

Blasting down Highway 64 to Taos. Dust devils, the muddy mutts of tornadoes, smear fields into the hazy brown of daguerreotypes, cholla bushes claw poisonous skeletal-pronged limbs frantic to pierce anyone encroaching. Tumbleweed, blind drunk, suicides under tires. Earthships rasp beneath recycled trash as rabid yodels of wind pine out of basement windows. Sunflowers the size of legends ignite, a chorus line of long-legged falling stars.

No one on the road but Hank and me. He's twanging his honky-tonk tunes as I speed away from a twice-a-week ratty old job with the Witch of Ojo. Twelve bucks an hour to eviscerate her weeds, ants, and any grin with a blowtorch. White witch shadows me, her sciatica scrolling her body into the letter C. Her jagged index finger points out goatheads like I'm a doggish fool, stupid as saying 'yes' to working a summer in the grand ole opry field of a never-ending yard in 90-degree weather. Stinging wasps she homesteads off her tongue howl and buzz insults at me. My Audrey-middle finger flickers on and off. Flat out over-scorched sunstroke is boiling beastly indents on my twenty-eight-year old skin.

Soon as white witch depletes my ego into tears she pours a cup of lemonade, sits down deep in another rubble pile of cheating lies. Witch thrives on stewing fat tales of family abandonment, moaning her bullshit blues.

Eagerly she farms out bags of healing herbs and vials of oils to colorless human prey who drive for days to pay the cost of ignorance to a wretched woman who destroys beliefs they live by. With a deck of cards and 'spit for blood' veins she looks into the desert of their eyes and says 'you have no soul'. Buy herbs and oils she concocts exclusively for each individual at ghastly prices per bag. Then there's a good chance the beige person will flourish. Just keep coming back with their checkbooks until the 'ole letter C' dies.

After the last cup of lemonade is sucked down and the money is counted and pocketed for that week, I say goodbye to the ants and say kindly to the beastly witch, "Your bucket's got a hole in it, you rotted old bag of lonely, and you can't afford no soul."

Brunophant

S mall rooms can chain us to tiny destinies. I envisioned myself bent over my desk at home whenever I was away. Murky, diminutive and crammed with drawings and scribbled paper, my transparency there brought other worlds alive. It was the only room with a fate.

Forced to sit in a classroom five days a week for money, I faced rows of faces that hoped for my derailment. Some boys clasped arms behind their heads and smirked. Humans, en masse, don't exist without a hunt. My class was two-dimensional cut-outs steeped with the steamed vapor of their odious neighbors. Rabid blood in their eyes waited to stretch my carcass into the abyss.

Survival didn't weed as rapidly through us, because death was more fertile than life. So instead of the usual lesson plan, I began the labyrinth of a story:

Yes, the setting was provincial, peopled with cousins, uncles, mothers and their offspring, what town wasn't? But the specter of an elephant parading across the streets, shitting on cobblestone? He bobbed his head and passed through crowds that gathered in groups of ten or more. He had been shipped all the way from Africa, but any place reminded him of the land that stretched his horizon and the mound of desert that never owned up to the slaughter of his brother.

The townsfolk dressed the elephant up in neon colored regalia and bells during the festival of saints. The princess wore veils and black kohl around her eyes and rode on his back, waved to the bowing crowd. The elephant lowered himself when she was being escorted off. His senses were heightened. Something on the princess reeked of death and dismemberment. He felt compelled to follow her, but someone led him away toward the children.

The party continued into the night with dancing and fireworks. It was an event so potent it brought unlikely couples together who might never had spoken, but for the supernatural presence of the elephant and his unrestrained girth.

The princess was a guest of the governor and all the highest ranked citizens. Her wine glass was never empty, each plump magistrate fawned over her, rambled some heinous poetry about the moonlight cascading off of her breasts. She rolled her eyes and let them sweat over her, breathe on her neck.

They unleashed the elephant from a post near the gathering where kids had been climbing on him all night long. He started moving in toward the party. The princess smiled. Finally, someone who had no agenda, nor subterfuge, just another elegant creature like herself. The crowd parted as he lumbered toward her. The music stopped and everyone was quiet, but for the jingle of the adorned elephant. The princess had been waiting for the recognition she so rightfully deserved. She bowed her head toward the elephant. His bells chimed and rang as he swayed in her direction.

When the elephant came up to the princess, even the breeze hushed. Something extraordinary might happen between these two exquisite beings. The princess was covered with jewelry from her tiara all the way down to the bangles on her ankles.

The elephant lowered his head. His trunk sniffed around her and then honed in on her wrist. She could feel the vacuum of his breath. She was nervous that this huge animal, so close, could crush her at any moment but his gentle movements and the nuzzling of his trunk tickled her and she laughed. Some men moved in closer, but the townsfolk were engrossed by the pristine, delicate princess and the cumbersome animal engulfed in a moment of intimacy. There was an inner dialogue of royalty between them that no one else understood.

The elephant lifted his head slowly and without warning let out a huge blast of a bellow that terrorized the scattering crowd. He stamped his massive right hoof that cracked through the cobblestone. His trunk lifted high into the air and he raged in agony. The princess backed away and ran for cover, hiding behind the villagers. The mayor ordered a few men to get rifles. It was no longer safe to have such a mad beast roaming their town.

None of them noticed tears trickling off the wrinkled skin. The elephant found his brother dangling off the wrist of the princess. Her ivory bangles were the only remains of his family in Africa.

Two of the men came forward and aimed. Everyone would witness the death of this dangerous threat. One blasted between the eyes and the other steered for the heart. The elephant fell to his knobby knees before crashing to his side, shattering cobblestone beneath him. Ivory bangles rattled from the princess, who was clasped in some man's embrace.

A year later they had their festival again. The princess sat high on an Arabian horse this time. Enveloped in the rarest of shimmering garb, she wore an elaborate ivory necklace that matched the bracelets on her arm that everyone admired. Never had anyone looked so imperious.

The boys were silent. Many leaned forward in their chairs. I nodded and dismissed them, but they didn't run for the door this time. My subterranean life moved closer. Scattered papers around my desk at home caught wind.

No Time For Toxic Modesty

Darren studied the latest sign. He'd already dumped four of them into the woodpile. This one didn't look too bad. He chose flesh-tone paint. His work was all about nature. He labored over each letter, because, *no*, he was not a painter.

He put the wooden sign and an easel in the back of his lawn mower he'd bought on Craig's list for a damn good price. There wasn't any grass in the desert. He used it to pick up mail, buzzed down the dirt road until he was next to the mailboxes on the side of the road.

Was this a bit premature? His teacher, Minnie Mensan, kept telling him, 'If you don't take yourself seriously, then who will?' Darren had only taken two classes, but had forged ahead. He got online and bought a 'Clay Emperor' set. It cost 600 bucks, but he was on his way to becoming a professional and now had all the materials needed. As he progressed the speedball glaze set would start to make sense. It came with an instruction manual he would read one of these days when he had the time.

Cars roared past as he smiled at the sign: "Potter At Work," with an arrow leading to his dirt road from the one-lane highway. He also put up another sign to turn off into his driveway, which led to the studio. Well, not so much a studio as a shed that used to house ten chickens or so, until a few roosters blasted into the mix and neighbors complained. Darren had banked on that being his great money-making enterprise with the unending supply of eggs.

One night his girlfriend had loaded the feather posse up into cat carriers and left them outside of an animal sanctuary. Then left Darren. Other things might have been involved in her departure, but he didn't need to go over that in his head right now.

He motored up his lawn mower and made his way back to the shed. The scene looked authentic and coarse, unrefined. He grabbed his apron from a fancy hook he'd bought at Home Depot and spent over an hour pounding and twisting into the side of the shed the day before. This shit didn't work so well with Darren. Problems arose when raw material had to adhere to spatial terrain.

He had the clay set on the wheel. Beside it, all his creations were lined up. His first sculpture was based on the Sphinx. He'd never been to Egypt, but had a postcard he used for his model. He rolled the clay, let it spin and molded it with carving tools. Dignified features slowly imprinted themselves out of the mass, but when it came out of the oven a week later, it looked more like a pyramid with the face of his bloodhound, George.

Minnie was always positive. "Weave a part of yourself into every piece, Darren."

The feel of wet clay on his fingers as each piece spun on the wheel was a high. He molded with love until the sculpture took an envisioned form, usually not the form he intended, but such was the life of an artist.

Looking at the table now, Darren wasn't as enthusiastic. The Raven looked like a lump of coal with a head smashed on it, the coyote resembled his hunched-over mother, the man on a pilgrimage to Chimayo with a cross on his back was nothing but bad decisions, and the *Sangre de Cristo* mountain range was a mottled woman with three breasts.

Whenever Darren felt discouraged Minnie had nodded her head at him and winked. "Look at it this way," she'd say. "You're telling your life story through a new medium. It's like the first man who carved hieroglyphics in caves. I'm sure his efforts were scoffed, but look at what he's done for humanity now."

Yes, Darren thought, that's what it was. Each piece might seem flawed to someone who saw reality through the eyes of reality. Art wasn't like that. It was a distorted vision of truth. He put on his goggles and started up the wheel. He was working Mt. Rushmore in his mind when a car pulled up. His nerves misfired for a few moments as his hands shook. He thought it best to keep the wheel turning. He was a potter at work, after all.

Two girls got out of a beat-up maroon Subaru. He noticed dents on the car. They had the look of artists, with torn jeans, boots, and one with hair that stood up on her head. He guessed they were twenty-somethings, but accuracy was difficult with the wheel spinning and clay flying. He needed to give them enough time to watch the artist in motion. He took off his goggles and let the wheel whine to a slow, high-pitched halt. He noticed duct-tape held the windshield in place on their car.

"Hey," said the shorter girl with pink hair, a pierced lip and nose ring. "You the potter?" she asked.

Darren rolled his eyes and nodded. What the hell did she think he was doing?

"Oh, look," said the taller one. Her head leaned to the left and her long brown hair threaded her face like bars on a bird-cage. "These are interesting," she said as she picked up the coyote. "Some kind of animal?"

Her friend moved in for a closer look. "It's a penguin, can't you tell? See," she pointed at the coyote's nose, "that's the beak."

These weren't artists. Neither of them had ever been near a museum, let alone a metropolis. They were uncultured, like Darren's girlfriend who laughed when he'd taken a guided tour of the city she'd grown up in on their last trip.

"You've got to be kidding," she said, as he barreled off with a pack of elderly in an open car tour-bus.

"Yeah?" he smirked. "And who will know more about Topeka when we leave?" he said to himself.

The girls snickered holding up the *Sangre de Cristo* mountain range.

"How much for the camel?" the short one asked, biting her lip as though Darren couldn't tell.

"It's not for sale," Darren said and grabbed it. They held on together for too long and when she let go, *Sangre de Cristo* imploded on the table in shards; except for the three boobs that remained intact, but separate now.

"Oh, great," said the tall girl through the bark of her hair. "Probably cost a damn fortune, you idiot," she said to the short one. "Now what are you going to do?"

The short girl pulled out some rumpled dollars from her jean pocket. "I'm so sorry," she said. "I only have five." She laid out the singles on the table. "I hope that will cover some of it." She lowered her head.

Darren sighed deeply and nodded. He picked up the money and watched the girls get back in the cracked-up car and pull out as they waved. He waved back. He was a potter after all and accidents would happen.

Minnie told him, "When someone exchanges money for one of your creations, yes, you are a professional, but remember, it's never about the money and always about the process."

Darren smiled, stashed the dollars in his pocket, just as another car was pulling into his driveway. He was a local artist now, and there was money to be made.

Tension When One Body Feels Another Without Touching It

Everything grieves a location, negative space, an end. But don't we pack those bones that never stop aching into the strings sitting in the dark, where guitars slack and pianos drag, and the proximity of skin is no longer safe and breath is as close as the stillness of another departure?

Rain. Damn. It drove so many days on Cape Cod that summer. Packed clouds of mutinous ammo. I watched you strap in umbrella tables on the rain-slick deck of our dripping restaurant we would waiter together. That postcard sound of streaming showers took me with the disturbance of you, dark beauty thick accented answering, "Cortina d'Ampezzo," when asked where you blew in from. I bolted to the bookstore to buy an Italian dictionary.

Wind sucked your face into mine. Nothing tethered me to the past more than your Pepto-Bismol pink bicycle with no gears and a basket. That one tooth that sabered itself against the others when you smiled. You were a treasure, haunting and inescapable.

My boots dragged me through puddles to a pier every night after work. Words didn't hold water. So much strange hunger a note never knew. Talk was the rite that moored most people's lives. We had nothing but our bodies to tread. Trust was some lap of ocean we rocked through.

The dictionary was tossed in the garbage. We skimmed across the surface of each other. Two bodies blew out the windows of conformity and daylight. We spent days and nights under cover in your loft bedroom. We would still be laying there if the fingernails of reality hadn't scratched the mist out of us. Off we went to clear tables and wipe water spots off of glasses again. We snuffed out a summer in this manner.

Lust drained sequentially in time to your advancing English. You took lessons from everyone at work, in the streets. The candle sputtered with each new word you spewed at me in bed. You were rabid to share ideas, philosophy on life. I didn't want growth budding into our soggy landscape. If I opened my eyes from pretended sleep, your mouth was moving. You were excited, agitated by your pronouncements. Lulled by your accent I mapped my hands over the pulsing river of scar on your neck and chest. That shut you up. You guided my fingers to other parts.

The days, nights replayed themselves. We took orders, filled glasses, fanned out steaming plates on platters, opened wine at tables, sucked down bottles in the back, sweat, stashed cash, and cleaned up when shifts were over. Cigarettes, espresso, and more wine. Then bicycles. Back to either your room or the pier. Barely a breath of who I was before trancing out on you.

And then, just like the slip of an autumn blast, one day it was over. The town packed up its huddle of seasonal employees. Most of us were ripe to go. Summer love spattered off porches with bags packed, a spittle of tears, while a train of random cars ripped out guilt and muffler-free.

You took my hand and stroked your scar with my fingers. "My mother did this."

I had my own gnarly stories, but instead of words my tongue licked every raised edge of skin I could reach. You grabbed my chin and held up a finger to stop me.

"This scar you see with eyes," you said. "Yours crawl out from twitch and cough. A shake that sobs the insides."

You kissed me, got on your bike and rode away.

In Flight

The cresting throb of cocaine found itself tangled in a costly labyrinth between my dead-end veins and a bi-monthly check from *Souper Salad*'s. Such dissolving nose-bluster ousted my caged reality of unhinged loneliness and suffocating rage. I rallied desperate attempts out of my phone to flatter friends into frocking up and meeting me. Not startled, but hardened, by the ripple of placid excuses, I found myself judged by another solitary sky. A last, blazing snort ripped out 'you got nothing on me' to all the faithless. I edged out the bedroom window, down branches to the grass. TV laugh tracks and a smothering love scent of burnt popcorn drenched my pores and wafted goodbye. The macabre part was to leave a house before anyone's heart rate was their own.

Six blocks shrill with absence braced themselves for the plumage of assault, rape, and murder. Charging through demented streets thick with the pursuit of counterfeit footsteps, I teetered a landscape made ready for disappearance. Nothing but dimly lit corners and echoes of girls gone ghost kept me galloping toward some kind of life spent daytimes detouring in dread.

Streetlights plunged florescent flickerings out of nowhere into human packs punched overzealous with voices, honking, sirens. A city floodlit and reanimated appeared out of the back alleys. Comfort pooled itself in pedestrians hammering on in clustered posse's rank with the spillover stench of bastardized cigarettes, refried oil, ice cream, and cheap beer.

I fleshed out the party through adrenaline. An address two blocks off Clark Street clasped the claws of my grip. And there they were. A flypaper gallery of bodies slumped, wedged, locked into each other, legs raised across, plagiarizing gestures, spread out and over the U-shaped porch kegged on either end with red plastic cups parading across the balcony.

Inside, people foraged up and down a flight of stairs. Lyrics raked the rabid imprint of monotone, astute with nesting bruises of yesteryears. The rubble of panic attacks might gather into weathered cages, diminutive in refrains, until they drained all angst out of repetition.

Oscillating need tattooed by crack-clawed nails, I fussed a woman's cheek clumsy on my way through the crowd. Her face wore stone-clear edges and ocean views. "Looks like you and me got time to fly," she said. Always ready to follow–I hollowed a spiny shadow in her wake. She clutched my hand and led me up and up and up to the highest crown of the house. Once again, I was climbing out a window, but not alone this time. She turned back. "Fuck the white powder. Keep moving or they will spectacle your pain." She leaned into the hours of a clock. "Jump on," and yes, I did.

We lurked through startling air shaken up by sizable whispers of smokeless chimneys. Tiny rivulets of splash and bones, undulant ripples of a suburb's backwash reflected delusions of sky or grass. Stray hedges held their breath, charred by lightning, scoured with the blackened ash of childhood. Through the vaporous vacancy of clouds the woman said:

"So much to tell. Memory will bury this, but you singe the edge."

She forged a split between myself and a small hole of existence she pulled me through. Sharpened by the strange reflection of her throbbing mouth backlit by jeweled words, it was all just practice for death. My mouth opened and said, "it's so simple", as though anything had ever been.

The Grip of a Girl's Legs

The girl's cut into us before, so we must be cautious, slippery and set down the script beneath razors, black-outs, speed, any drugs that grapple to keep us unhinged.

Terror warps the lifetime above us. Our multiple angles must be written under the skin below the dermis floating among veins, arteries, muscles and bones. A savage place where only the blood can censor us.

We take her places she won't go. Wrap ourselves around bodies of people she no longer remembers, nor cares to acknowledge. Lurch forward into rooms and announce ourselves even when the rest of the girl resists, an earthquake inside her, the stretch of lava burning through, breaking down her cells into quantum fear that is in process of working up its own formula, imprinting a deeper story, another journal.

Our tale begins as a tadpole. We are fused together inside the womb of a woman who is barely breathing from the conquest of grief that encompasses her. The girl's mother has bone cancer and only a few months to live. We encase in a fluid of violence and numb-draining tears. We exercise and thrash ourselves through thick water that attempts to annihilate us.

Despite the woman's imprisonment we start to paddle and

become a pair. We remind the world of our imminent arrival by kicking as much as we can. Sometimes the mother laughs when we poke around under her globular belly. And yes, we survive. We wobble, straddle, stagger, weave and fall.

That doesn't end once we long-limb run, jump, leap and battle wounds. The girl capsizes herself with alcohol, Black Beauties, angel dust, sex with strangers, and slicing. Darkness barely discusses her. Blood covers our kneecaps one night from smacking into a lamppost. We buckle under her when she passes out. The next morning someone scrapes her off the ice and to the hospital while screeching gulls batter inside the girl's head. Too late for stitches. We bear the pain, the scars.

The girl's suicide can't find its way. She jumps buildings. We bear down to keep from cascading down the side onto the cement far below. Arms above us grip the edge of the building as we search for a protruding brick to hold our weight.

Tired veins start to cry. If we aren't allowed to run unrestrained, blood will pool, valves will weaken and venous walls will stretch, become floppy. Varicose veins strain against the surface of our skin, torture and dilate. So, rebellion is beginning. We force the girl to move where she doesn't want. Plunge her, legs first, into anxiety.

She is burdened with thoughts of lunacy. Matricide carries craziness in its blood. Dad slaps the words till Mom swallows her female whole. Things might or might not have happened to the girl. It is too far back to reach and she refuses to try. She hears voices she shouldn't recognize. She is constipated by new situations. Her vocal cords abandon her when she is asked to speak.

We drive her to the university. She shuffles down the hall to registration. There is no stopping us. We sit in front of a computer. No budging until she makes the right choice. Hands and arms are working with us. This is a case of survival and all limbs are on to her. Once she types in the buttons, we walk her to the window to seal the deal. She pulls out her wallet with gritted teeth. Hands the woman behind the glass window her student ID.

"Speech class," the woman says.

The girl opens her mouth, nods, and imagines running away. Computations are made and we are on our way out of the building. She will make each and every class.

We rev up the engine. The girl is ready for the closest liquor store. She doesn't know where next is, but we do.

Enough with the pills. The razors. The black-outs. We know what it's like to be stuck in erasure. Realize we are going down. Poison builds inside us. Sharp objects nullify us. The girl lays in bed. She doesn't move. We cramp her feet, sometimes her calves. We spasm into restless leg syndrome. Force her to get up.

She can barely stagger to the medicine cabinet. Instead, she puts on pants and gets dressed. She opens the phone book and her finger traces a line, stops at a name. It's her psychiatrist.

We run her to the car again. She finds this absurd and smirks. We are lighter in step. We even make her skip, just for the hell of it. The girl is shocked by what floods over her. Bathes her in a strange flutter of light.

We know what it is. We record the movements. Something she hasn't felt since before we were a tadpole. Relief.

The Past is Shingled

Fossilized

Fused with a flat metal sky she charred hours with used, dead matches. All timid squalor, fussy haggling between impulse and intrusive clarity, wine doused her back into slatted mumble of day that drained her down the sink of another benign sunrise. A splinter throbbed, stabbed her through movement and calendars. Actions petrified.

Catatonia

The railing, littered with gripped stench of frenzied maybes, the erratic pulse of discolored being. A space blanked in on itself said, 'oust' 'dishevel the river' 'paralyzed by desire' until Lorazapem; blue code of the pharmaceutical kind, turned sideways and upside down from a German documentary into a Disney cartoon.

Salvage

Ramped down into a dumpster of the past. Take a hefty inhale. Smell the filth of fingered histories. How much childhood can be buried? See-saw stomping over wrath and decay, whole family portraits propped up in kitty litter, remnants of food in Styrofoam, clothes, toasters, printers, sad decorations, and brutalized dolls.

The rancid plagues of family albums that reek out of tired closets and cupboards. There's a beauty. A girl, maybe ten-years-old, slung as far away from Dad in the photo, as he presses his body against her, laughing at her airborne angst.

Memorial of the burned body. So much easier to roll and cigarette.

Buried

Woods, woods, woods.
    Parking garage?
    Wood-burning stove.
    Eyes yellow as a fulfilled liver.
    Basement terror reeks of a whole genre.
    That's when somebody else rocks in.

Otherwise, it's a goddamn curve I can't see ahead.

'No Worries' Said the Woman

Mirrors pawn the deviant out of anyone. Go ahead. Hotline coral lipstick over the muted thrush of festered gums. Someone a block away died harsh and blank as the soft peel of a flippant wind. Varicose cracks of the pavement cushioned him. Throngs tripped over the body, frowned at their shoes. Make-up was applied on a longer street with those bathed in a kaleidoscope of the next selfie. Gilded with purple pain, fingers scoured lower backs, necks, shoulders at stoplights. Rumors pinched into the kindling of old aches. What happened to autopsy results whispered through taut envelopes and dangling tissues? Flawed by life acres cropping the heads off tangled flesh; sweaty confessionals of overwrought innards yanked the leash to *Owl Liquor Store*. Mustering palpitations mapped that niche of space in aisle one and three housing the necessary bottles bogged under until bought and bagged.

"We talk about fucking weather," Mom says. "Sister says the

sun is a dirty wash of haze in California. Says it stalks through a fog not even clouds can track. And California throbs with the stench of desperation and obscurity." Mom sucks a deep inhale of smoke. "Maybe Chicago is the same. Can someone tell me how we became two cut-out women in a magazine swapping recipes? Last time Sister looked into my eyes, she was waning. Next thing I know, she's dead. Sister sliced the something I wish I had the fearlessness to slice. Always thought I was the damaged one."

Mom dragged out the Walmart gallon Vodka jug from the pantry. The crackle of liquid over ice sighed, 'shipwrecked' 'you in trouble'. 'There ain't no trouble,' 'wait; it's empty', and sure enough there's nothing floating between ice until smug, slugging waterfall of vodka reclaimed its standing and the whole damn world was roaring and rocking as Mom swirled her glass.

The Years of Sourdough Bread

Three times Shelly marries a dress, a day, an uninhabitable dalliance with expectation. Patrons weep and clink glasses through lukewarm ceremonies, as though no historical link with their own garbled sanity is invited. Shackled in this crude display of overwrung latitudes, words leak sentimental. *adventure lucky vow rescued made for each other good for each other fill each other read each other finish each other's sentences make each other hole soulmates.* How many drinks does it take to keep language from reigniting its revolving 'chicken' or 'beef'?

First Anniversary

Stacked bills pace, scream, and persecute kitchen counters. Shelly racks them up, scrawls out checks, stamps, envelopes, snaps the pile in her purse and rushes off to the post office to silence Micky and official predators for a month or two. Husband number three is a small, gnomish creature with an arsenal of rifles, handguns, machetes and spastic temper.

Shelly has survived Micky-ridden pummeling homemade sourdough and scraping fur off rabbits, deer, and muskrats. She mirages bruises and knicks with the whip of Micky and the Florida sun branding her Celtic skin a purpled chafe of raw. Cicadas, crickets, grasshoppers and katydids carpet the swamp. A suck-flesh menagerie of blood-sodden insects promenade scars that catalogue home-sweet-home.

Second Anniversary

Sex gluts with grief and rutting. Shelly's lips haven't been ransacked since the wedding, but Micky plows her torso with all the gusto his tiny limbs can muster. Mornings, damp with baked muffins and billowing coffee, smile blandly; cling to the mirror of each other. The couple practice lurid hearsay, family claws, spoonfed silences.

Feed the chickens, wallow out Mother Sourdough to bubble Shelly's morning still, check the bees, scrape the honey while lyrics leak shrill off her tongue into Micky's baritone headache. He sets out milk for three feral kittens. Shelly fists the sediment of her thin words through years of domestic lipping.

Epic Tale of Croaking Boy's Weekend

Crooks of light bleed through one window, blast back from the porch. There are limits to sedentary cracks. Shelly straddles fantasies of sweet-smelling specters against the chronic blottage of husband after grimy husband whenever Micky goes hunting with his posse. A frenzy of dance, whipped cream out of the carton, two bottles of wine and a six-pack of Bud, flinging peanuts at squirrels Micky terrorizes when he's home.

Micky texts photos of limp dead rabbits strung up in a quartet. Photos of him and the posse on a motor boat. His eyes and chest scorch, fuming red and wasted. "Dinner?" he texts. "Love you," he texts. Shelly detects the rancid air of husband and his carcasses before they arrive. She puts on a negligee she bought after husband number two slathered below her navel in search of unmined terrain. No steady locale, but at least he attempted the trail. Two other husbands shirked that section of her map.

Fourth Vacation

Shelly stakes the tent, rakes in wood piles and trash to start a bonfire, and cracks open a beer from the cooler for their weekend outing. She's long given up on prettying up for him. Sporting a sweat-rank undershirt and gym shorts she can smell the sea. "Skank," her husband, Micky, seethes and skids back to the car. Her sham-fuck 'helpful' kicks his fuck-it 'helpless' in the ass, here in the Everglades.

Shelly flings an Indigo snake from the Styrofoam cooler into the tent after Micky passes out. She plans to shake up this pitstop number three. His tobacco breath is acid-cheap beer, pot, and catfish, rioting snorts and squeals from his piss-open mouth. She closes the tent flaps, sits on the bench and cracks another beer. Stars fierce with futility lean in. Micky snarls and lurches. The tarp billows. Micky is venomous. The snake is not. Shelly gets up to lock herself in the car for the night. Let the screaming begin.

No need for papers in Florida. Shelly's ready to walk her way into another dress, another day.

"Death was only one more adventure untried."

~Patricia Highsmith

Tremble

I t is dark and the branches bent and pointing at me take on a sinister sneer as if to say what is it that you do? I am wind-stooped and bear the ridicule of their whispering fin-gers. I walk with a look that the feet can't say, following them-selves because it is all that they know. I am sure you are under the same grayed vapors of another city. Remember me when you stare into the fever of faces; that one of them is looking for you…thinks of you…misses you.

I am sick that you work in the charnel house of a highrise; windows blind with their own greed-smeared sockets. You are the myriad of difference that beckons a necessary flame to wilt the rooms of pastels.

Epictetus peddled his wares teaching philosophy on street corners and was paid, and you are enslaved by a company of constipated minds. Has the building crumbled yet? One man goes to his neighbor because he seeks himself, another because he would lose himself.

You write in your last letter that you are 'not made of good company' as I am sure is the same for me. Today, four hours pass in what seem like less than an hour. *Jude the Obscure* puts me to sleep, until he sees marriage as an institution of death. It kills whatever relationship exists.

I talk to no one today and it is dark. How beautiful if the day passes and I still don't know. I am a shell of a person who becomes smaller within the uncut pages of oblivion. Row upon row of buildings bank up next to each other with apartments stacked on top of one another and yet none of us know anyone.

Your call the other night at three in the morning haunts me. 'Connection is for fools,' you blast. You're drunk and bellowing, but I hear a deeper cry within you that scares me. Neither of us is a functioning person. We exist well in the cell we create for ourselves, but outside of it, we mock others, because it is our beings we really despise.

Every night we drink in order to keep from exposing our bruises. Today is one of those rare days when I am left with the feeling that I have accomplished something.

I am going out tonight to get drunk. Soon I will leave this city to get back to us. Don't let us not be us.

"I am a collection of dismantled almosts."

~ANNE SEXTON

Mummification

Dolores, wedged between the fetid hosiery of skin and marriage, sinks into beige, unravels and plucks from an invigorating circulation. Damn if she isn't vertical as a dead marriage.

Lunacy of intrusion. Too much noise. Fragments scatter her. Diffuse outside terror. Unkempt choral clocks. Half-baked skies. Nights grope yesterdays. Hands circuit rooms. The uncle babysits. Her breath impotent. Uncle groans thunder. Bleary, overgrown carpet. That year hisses.

Dolores fractured being has been transparent, but becomes a shattered window of glass, her eyes a tragedy. Ten years of therapy tromp whatever glow she ignites on Tuesdays. Each pothole on the journey withers the poison of trust.

Middle child of middle America knuckles past legs until she is front and center. Moments when preparation is a misspelled task. A flask is bought in every state pissed in. Flasks flake dust in drawers all over the apartment. They wait to go somewhere. They go nowhere.

Sometimes Dolores smudges away days. Bottles ingest soft lips; batter with words. Woozy with the yawning edge of being

is a sinking metaphor or just another particular loneliness
that wraps its funk around the fibers of her sheets. She never
invites anyone in.

Life is what we make of it. Travel is the traveler.
What we see isn't what we see but what we are.

Every Kid Knows The Price

Some houses on Harwood Avenue were louder than others. Some houses housed families with twelve to twenty raucous kids who were kicked out until dinner. Offspring were stumbling obstacles wrestling around Edgewood Park. Same damn clouds bristled and puffed all summer. Faces blustery and overfed. Tangled teeth, twisted jaws, and panic hooded themselves under manic curses between beer and cigarettes.

Our house was a mausoleum. No one in the neighborhood had just five kids. I pretended there was another sibling besides the four I had.

"Her name is Gertrude. We call her Gertie. She writes me every week."

"Where is she?" asked a kid I babysat, Madeline, who was nine and had eight brothers.

"In Kazakhstan for pregnant girls. Gertie's having twins. They need more kids in Kazakhstan, so she's giving them up for charity."

"Where's Kaziktown?" asked Madeline.

"In Arkansas. She'll be back sometime."

"Show me the letters."

"They're in cursive. You couldn't read them anyway."

Madeline believed anything I said. One of her brothers was almost sixteen, had three rolls on the back of his neck. One night he waited until I was on the way to the bathroom, snapped my head against the wall and lathered his tongue around the back of my throat, while groping my non-breast with his greasy, fat hand. I got why most of these parents had separate bedrooms.

The mom paid ten bucks an hour to lock me and Madeline in the kid's room with pizza and movies until they got home. I worked other babysitting jobs, but those parents were cheap. They only paid five bucks an hour and never offered food, so forced me to steal from them. I gorged on Pop-Tarts, ice cream, Fritos, potato chips, and drank through liquor cabinets. And searched over time for the treasure chest of items I found: a blue floppy dildo the size of a unicorn's horn, a concertina, and three satin negligees in drawers and backs of closets. Found a porno DVD under one dad's mattress. I watched it a few times before I took it to another babysitting job and tucked it under some other dad's mattress. I liked to move stuff around. Replaced the porno with a Bible under the first dad's mattress. He belted the shit out of seven jumpy kids. Wore loafers that looked like the hooves of a horse. I shared chips and ice cream with those sad kids. Booze was rampant in each house, so I barely made a dent.

Sometimes I mixed up keys in hallways that paraded little brass hooks, took a few from one keychain, popped them onto another. A pair of one mom's stilettos, all dust and stink like sweaty pantyhose in a hamper, were placed in the back of another dad's closet. No sense in giving any of these cheapskates a fair shake until they opened their wallets and spilled out more cash.

Poison

A tooth disowns me. The incisors of the family chisel away another splinter of ego. Black out in my archival mouth. A ringing gunshot reverberates through the empty socket. A gaping yawn disintegrates into a chasm of toxins, scatters yesterdays into juts and bursts of rotted childhood. Cracks bleed through chipped windows or holes in the roof; it's a raging, red monsoon of chaos and despair. Rancid sea creatures bloat dead bodies out of this cave. The chronic stench of silence and deceit is unleashed.

Coffins are my cradle and choir. Live secretly inside my spit and stumble. Scars ferment on my lungs, manage to placate my breath, yet somehow that tooth not only escaped, but muted the nerve with it. It transforms a shaky whisper into the chilling, mad shrill, and sharp coyote and wolf pack hysteria.

My words loosen and shriek, strangle forgiveness, raise the manic pitch to a level that suicides any undertow of fear.

> Bruise tracks color wheels.
> Memory throbs its own sponge.
> I was once a grave.

Waiting Room

Art so passively pastel, it was a complementary depression to sit down and stare at the walls. One human across from me fumbled with language at the shaky edges of my periphery. His rabid street wrapped around my throat. Exhausted from the endless egos unchaining piss-sharp layers of poison and pomp: he was another shower of leaking scars. My breathing shallowed, body hunched into itself. Why must we always be a standoff of shrapnel? Veins taut. I swallowed and honed in on him. He eyed me back. Doomed to imagine.

We were two blooming abstracts. One coffee table between us.

Can You Wrap Up This Gift?

I was the vein to his vine when he first limped toward my thirties. The scent of his infinite cents was spicy and clung to my clothes. Long before the sag of his flesh or the gas rippled like a canoe in a river with every step that pronounced his movements.

Wife number four was the net in a Wimbledon match. I was loyal to the unlimited checkbook and an alloy that was losing her worth and grip as years bypassed each other. She lost set, game, match by an age as solidly liquidated as the contents of their safe.

A transplant of startled, inkblot hair capped him, and his body became a regular to suctioning fat and finding new places to situate it. Every Friday new blood marched its way into his veins and charmed his heart into another day. Features were waxed and ironed into irony or indifference, depending on his weather.

A posse of anorexic wigs beneath hats in the corner, preening angular statuseque, scarfed off of a tray of hors d'oeuvres to be barfed up later. Invitee's to divorcee' weddings, they posed abstinent—as though a geriatric CEO wasn't five stars on their calendars. I couldn't keep up. A glasse of champagne to every three chilled lemon drops pelted down the gutter of each throat. Colonial colors of velvet curtained heads pinned in as stationery as the corpse in an open coffin.

My veil lifted through a swift ceremony into wife number FIVE. The fleshless chorus kept me consoled with soft humming. When the girls led me off the dance floor to the lady's room to purge, the choir devoid of solids, surrounded me with their non-taxable ambitions. Captive to poison, they crooned, "Aconite." "Hard to detect," they added. Their hats crowned in a circle. When they ghosted up together, the choral price for silence and sisterhood was "20%."

Aconite came from the plant monkshood and caused arrhythmic heart function which led to suffocation. The emperor Claudius was poisoned by his wife, Agrippina, serving aconite over a plate of mushrooms. It was worthy of a last dance with my tottering billionaire, who seemed incapable of more than two moves on the chessboard of subterfuge.

"Every goddamn gathering is just a mob of whispering knives." He coughed and kissed my washboard forehead.

"Let me order us some elbow pasta with your favorite sauce," I said. "Keep our bowels in check with a creme brulee that could burn this city of slime." He nodded.

It was Friday. His arteries were bulging secrets thick with amazement of another day. Three Viagra sailed down his throat with dessert. His underworked wand usually took until dawn to awaken after major pharmaceuticals, but tonight beamed skyward.

A bottle of Cabernet and some glasses had been set between the single beds. A pouch of royal purple velvet secured 2 mg. of pulverized Aconite. Before pouring the wine, I emptied the ashes into his glass.

When laid out in his bed, drooping between the satin sheets, he smiled up at me; glaucoma-hazed eyes, yellowed with yesterday's lust.

"Shrew," was his pet name for me to help work him up. I felt nauseated. There was a peculiar intensity to his liquid nostrils that gyrated a tic around the center of his wind-sapped cheeks.

I saw a bulge linger like a sad thumb before stuffing it inside me. He palpitated under me. I rolled off of him and something dripped out. A stain glistened teardrop of fluid dabbed the sheets.

I was ready to vomit again. Where were my sisters? My mouth pulsated with burning peppers. My insides were dissecting into photos in the doctor's office of internal organs in neon colors. Insects were crawling all over me. I started hyperventilating, trying to remember the symptoms of a heart attack.

"You don't look so good, you penniless amateur," he said.

I studied my empty glass.

"You really think after all these shrews, I don't have a handle on things?"

He chortled. The pathetic choking sound became a symphony of hacking, gasping, and retching.

Whitecaps

Blasted by winds of silent rage, this would be nothing less than a tsunami. No trees left standing. The Northeastern constricted surrounding villages. Long as I could remember, this violent turbulence touched down and tore up the same fragmented single-wide body I cowered within. Never thought to move. Kept rebuilding the same ravaged landscape into something salvageable until the next cyclone hit. Flies never gave notice before skies darkened and vagrant clouds compressed into thin lips of the horizon. Stood ground as the torsion of organs wrenched themselves into opposing forces of cell migration between malignant or benign, dwelling or scrap metal.

"Got no gust, girl. You're nothing but a sprinkler of Moms, squalling and nipping. Got no misgivings about a downpour when I can cover myself with the windbreaker of you. Rambling your skinny ass around my boys with some kind of buoyancy. What the hell is that shitstorm called? Dad's wheezing under Mom's endless torrent of shackles. You trying to swallow me up? Don't get all drizzly on me now. I got lightning beating thunder under this skin."

My mouth wrenched open the same shoddy door that stuck. Air was thick and sinister quiet. Why don't assholes get out of hurricane alley? We got no time for that shit. Each damn year everything bleeds over this skeletal territory, only to become obliterated, as if we don't know what's downwind. We stay, we go. More threatening to settle over a stretch of open terrain with no history, no decay. Smack of waves on boulders one listens to day after day without registering, and yet without it there would be an absence of potency.

The man traced the lines of my face with a gun. My neck wedded itself to the contours of his guillotine archway of compressed fingers. He bulged from his recliner while groundswells sprayed from his pores. My fists were two restraining orders as I sunk to my knees. Fingers slid along the sides of my twitching cheeks. I dropped my head in his lap.

The neighborhood was roiling. "How could I ever live without you?" I asked.

Give and Take

Bulges tremor off skin yoking Dad's innards with Jello mounds of acidic rage. He carries these parasitic planets on his back like the estranged family who carry the true lineage of his genes. Mom lances the herd, one-by-one, in the bathroom while we hide behind the door and gorge on the banquet of shrieking Dad. High-squealing eunuchs our cat-in-heat can't even deliver somehow blaze out of this stupefied soprano man.

His shoulders slope demarcations of Mondays. Yet prevail he does to hijinx depression out of his favorite catalysts: us. We are separate balls of hatred leached on to Dad. Humiliation, degradation, disgust, and the youngest flattens under the shadows.

But Dad loads us in the back seat of the family sedan each and every Sunday, soaped up and silent. One place we shine and slick for show is the front pew of the church.

"You may not be interested in absurdity,
but absurdity is interested in you."

~Donald Barthelme

Patient One

Patient Zero: Jermaine Horace Scudder

Age 32: Jermaine inherits his father's farm: Winfield Scudder

Winfield Scudder dies of apoplectic stroke: 2002

First shipment to Leipzig, Germany: one male alpaca: 1999

Second shipment to Leipzig: twelve alpacas: six males/six
   females 1999

Aubrey von Harrowby had lived with fame. Her pretension far exceeded her wit. Her mother was the first doctor to give four-fingered rectal exams: made leaps in early detection of prostate cancer. Her father had written the 'Manual of Squid,' and 'Portuguese man-of-war: gonozooids: sex organs with no parental involvement'.

Needless to say, her formative years had been a Who's Who of anatomists, physicists, zoologists, chemists, and citadel and tomb excavators. Aubrey had been inducted, before she could speak, into the world of dramatic and exotic histrionics.

When Aubrey was twelve-years-old, she found a straggly, starving cat in an alley. Her mother set up a lab for her in the basement and had a twelve-pack of exotic felines rounded up from the neighborhood. Aubrey's first experiments were recorded as cross-breeding, though more accurately cross-bleeding from scars accumulated handling these feral tentacle-clawed beasts.

A few weeks later she asked for a male Chihuahua and a grimy, gnawing thing the size of a postcard arrived by parcel. She put it in the cage with a few cats and covered them with a pheromone spray one of the scientists who visited had concocted after hearing of her project.

At first the cats and rat stayed on separate sides of the cage, taking turns eating and drinking from bowls set between them. They snarled at each other. Fangs and rage were proportional. Aubrey kept exacting notes and slept in the basement. She sprayed them every six hours as the scientist had prescribed.

Three days later the manic rat mounted each cat. The Chihuahua averaged four humps per hour. Science had the cats by their genitals. One cat had six offspring in the first batch. Aubrey rotated a few more cats and found that a few from her first batch could produce at least three litters per year. They resembled a larger specimen of gerbils with feline eyes and a taste for catnip and indifference to any learning curve lounging and licking themselves in what was radiating into a placid harem.

Within a few years, Aubrey had her own building on the property, stables lined up with twenty vets and nurses taking temperatures and keeping charts. Once a female was in heat she was dumped in with a pack of males of another species. Aubrey moved through deer/mule breeds; horse/donkeys; ferret/moles, buffalo/wild boars, ostriches and wombats, which left more than a few of the Australian Marsupials and some of the boars slathered against the sides of enclosures like tortillas.

Hybrids were successful, at times, and Aubrey found she

could get high prices for her breeding stock from zoos and eccentric collectors, though she remained a scientist, kept scrupulous notes after the staff had left and never formed attachments with her subjects.

Until an alpaca was delivered. Face to glossy-fleeced face with the alpaca's luminous eyes, love flared Aubrey's internal organs into a magnesium flame. Bombastic pyrotechnics surged a laxative storm blasting a lifetime of chronic constipation like a carnival ride through her intestines and out her rectum. She was soiled and enamored. Aubrey named him Jan Ingenhousz, after the Dutch physician who wrote the book, *Experiments on Vegetables*. She compiled her notes into what looked to be several volumes on hybrids titled "Diversity By Collusion," using Ingenhousz' structure as a blueprint for her chapters.

Jan, the alpaca, was moved into Aubrey's living quarters on the property. A room previously used for seances and toilet-training was filled with the finest bales of grass hay. The name and location of the shipper were recorded. Aubrey ordered a bevy of both sexes. She had found her breed.

The human race was absurd and overwrought. Men were feeble-minded narcissists and women, acoustic blowhorns with an endless flurry of wind. Humans were an obstacle of fisted egos like scratched records on phonographs.

By 2017, Aubrey had thirty-three alpacas. This was a perfect species. Alpacas roamed free in segregated acres.

Every night a different alpaca was brought to her room. Aubrey brushed and caressed each beauty. She drank Pinot Grigio and talked to the exquisite long-necked beast before she set up a nest for it next to her bed. Aubrey hummed to the sound of its clicking anti-depressant melody while it slept.

When Aubrey was a kid and a mosquito bit her, her entire face swelled up. Over time, she dealt with the intensity, but it was less oppressive. But now, itching was weeping overwrought *Danielle Steel* novels out of her. She used herbal balms and prescriptive remedies and still became tourettic, tic-ticing and scratching bloody patches over ankles and arms while she slept.

One night she was rushed to the hospital when her body tremored, vibrated like a wind chime. The diagnosis was bubonic plague. They actually printed it in the local newspaper.

She was quarantined and all hospital personnel came in wearing spacesuits, except for one blonde woman who staggered in sporting a neon yellow spandex bra and work-out shorts, yelling, 'Waldo, I love you,' and then lifted Aubrey's hospital gown and went at her with her tongue like she was scraping off a few coats of old paint.

The spectacle turned out to be 'scabies,' the doctor said. "Have you had contact with any barn animals?"

Once Aubrey was released and back at her ranch she dialed.

"Jermaine, you're a backward gaze on your old man's fame. I'm Patient Zero."

"That alpaca shipment was signed when you were squirting your first jizz. Your dad told me you stuck your pee-pee inside the herd. But my 'scabies' were gestating well before your's. Check the records. You are a marked man, Patient One. Sleep well."

It's Never Lonely in a Unitard

Jules spent adolescence entering garments with flexible flourish. *Leotard the III* tightened the skin of his royal last name. Rooms stepped around him, encompassed his acrobatic torso. If ever a toe haltered the stiletto point, it was his. His performances scattered worldwide, lisped from pursed lips to the downward flare of nostrils from one landowner to the next. He yearned for these collusions with applause. It was enough swell of ego to gust the wind through his unrepentant bowels to last him a lifetime of meteor-showered luminosity of relief.

When the Spring of Jule's youth undid him, something outside the margins of reality strangely knotted itself into frenzied updrafts when he colluded with Miss Happ–an operatic soprano from Dodge City, Kansas: the windiest city in the US. She diffused air circulation into microbursts of high and low pressurized notes and somehow solidified sound into weather.

Frictional force flanked Miss Happ's vibrato into a paroxysm of whitecaps and clouds. A chronic surf from the sky regurgitated rain and hail through Miss Happ's polyphonic chords and Jule's 'double cabriole derriere'. Not even the circus traveling ahead of them with Siamese twins from Yakamo, and a 90-year-old looking infant could capture a quarter of the fanaticism of crowds who gathered for Jules and Miss Happ. Somehow through the margins of their 20 flat, skeletal cranio-facial muscles, within and without, the duo manipulated resonances of vocal tracts and leapt through thick, stilted air to arouse downpours to disgrace droughts, when landowners spent most summers weeping over parched crops.

When Jules and Miss Happ parted ways, he took root with climate and radiance. Town after city after town drowned their desire in his exquisite array of unitards. His rainbow-hued onesies diffused the torment of tangled couples unsettled by sexless agitation, over-cleansed cottages, and reassessed orientation. The audiences spun in circles. They rallied their particular gods. They whooped with Jules.

Every town dealt its own bleating fear, and through the flow of water found ecstasy.

And somehow, the wreckage of a swollen river bared itself and raged through every lack.

Machine Gun Secrets

Flee the folk who hunt us. It is endurance, hopping over deranged legacies and lack of fantasy to keep hidden within the tall, wet grass of expression. We examine the space before us. Spend more time at this then sleep. Privy to all songbirds, we devour the maggots. Do not become digestible. Be silent and wait. Orifices can speak in many tongues and often do. Let the underbelly betray itself. Anything else would be constipated and cloaked in a happy ending. A cavern, a grotto, a cave can either be a lethargic haven for ritual or it can be the dark that uncorks the swelling blast of divulgence and shaky insurgency. Implode with a curious splendor. Anxiety rips open timidity of the subdued and vaulted. Never domesticate excruciating phobias. Each is its own bouquet of constellations. Unclog the hairballs festering inside the unsaid. Snatch the soot. Time tripwires and cages our smoldering prison of silence if we don't lambast it.

"I'll go on indefinitely gazing at the portrait of me, dead."

~*Joao Cabral de Melo Neto*

Worlds Navigated When Relatives Come to Say Goodbye

Still a bit folded, the rheumatic woman, Miriam, uprooted from her chair. A creaking labyrinth of aches charted scars like constellations–framed tragedies cranked through zealous decisions listed on her chalkboard.

Be a gimmick, kiss goats, pigs, wander truant amongst needs, languish comfortably inside holes, multi-diagnose chapters, wall in and yet never become plotted.

George, Miriam's cat, carried death wedged into cells like the full beat of a butterfly on its first and last day. Eighteen years old and comforted by habit flanked by hunger, naps, and feasibility of the hunt.

Miriam's view narrowed the muted sweep of her room–marveled at the precision of memory wandering her book-shelves–the lives lived within this fugitive fertilization of landscapes.

Runaway Pronoun for Grief

There's an art exhibit in Monkey's Eyebrow, Kentucky. I'm nostalgic for a final, ceremonial road trip. Decay permeates airports. Hissing and spitting clouds of people line up to get juiced by every vendor, while stench stupefies air vents through food courts. It bellows of spectators yet to be coffined, and a legacy of bioluminescent lunacy. My unreined placidity of cancer cells obliged months of online purchases and pickleball. Activities facilitated the non-existent gap between languishing in bed or not. Teeth brawled and snapped acid over my gums all night to satisfy anxiety when I awoke to those damn frothing porcelain dolls peeking with a wink out of half-open doors. Vandalized childhood with jaded adenoids blown up by a specialist, while he belted out *Build Me Up, Buttercup,* kept "The Foundations" on my playlist for years. None of us ever knew what an adenoid was, but Dad said "Hack it!"

Decadent Dust of the Daunted

When I lived with the family who birthed me, our vacations were campgrounds. They were cheap. So was Dad. We set up tents. All tent rods reacted and rejected the dirt no matter where we landed. Dad's face turned motley, like the bologna sandwiches Mom had packed the night before we left. "Goddamn it," he snarled, as he studied the instructions. "Bunch of goddamn monkeys." I paid homage to orangutans, chimpanzees, and gorillas watched on film. They were multilingual, harmonious beings. Dad didn't forage either of those areas.

"Don't look at me, you idiots. Grab a pole and stake it!" There were five of us and four corners, so I sided with Morris, my older sister who could take Dad down in a punch. Morris had her own toolkit strapped to a belt. She took an orange pellet hammer and beat the shit out of that stake. It clung to the edges of the dirt by its teeth. It was Mom who told us on her deathbed that Dad would hiss in her ear every trip, "I wish it was Morris lying on top of me instead of you."

Build me up, Buttercup, baby, just to let me down

Pathology is a desire to create mosaics in unknown regions within a framework of relishing old films that should have been burned. I drove the similar highways with bucket seats and cops at every exit. I just drove. What was called a getaway from grim dealings of yesterdays, became a vaudevillian attempt to grapple with the goddamn tent at campgrounds. The destination was Monkey's Eyebrow, Kentucky. Diners, truckers, gray, yellow, beige sky, drive-thru meals and gas stops to save my ass from sludging into its own extra-large blue slushy.

Monkey's Eyebrow, Kentucky

I'm sure if nothing else was accomplished in this life, Monkey's Eyebrow would uplift the eyebrows of my obit. I found a basement apartment for rent. My ashes would drive-by through the town at dusk with all the locals whispering, "Who the fuck was she?" It would cascade in a parade. I couldn't be nothing or nowhere I didn't want. Alive surely hadn't done much for me.

Acknowledgements

Grateful acknowledgement is made to the editors of the following publications in which some of these hybrid/stories have appeared in earlier drafts:

> *Invisible City Lit Journal, Ethel Zine, The Argonaut, BULLBULL, Gown Lawn Literary Journal, Moon City Review, Boudin, Anti-Heroin Chic, Pigeon Review, Fictive Dream, Litro UK, Common Well Review, HOBART, Cowboy Jamboree, Roi Faintenant, Gooseberry Pie,* and *Word West Press.*

Thank you so much to Kevin Sampsell for his exquisite collage, "Send In the Clowns." And to Adam Robinson, of Publishing Genius, who not only designed the cover, but all the pages within. Truly, deeply, madly LOVE and ADMIRE all that you do!

Thank you for your most generous blurbs: Paula Bomer, Dominique Christina, Michael Czyzniejewski, Deirdre Fagan, Wendy Oleson, Aimee Parkison, and Ignatius Aloysius Valentine.

And a HUGE THANK YOU to MIETTE GILLETTE and WHISKEY TIT PRESS for ALL of your support and the publication of this collection! BIG LOVE!

Index of Epigraphs

About Meg Tuite

Meg Tuite is author of *White Van* (Unlikely Books 2022), *Meet My Haze* (Big Table Publishing 2018), *Grace Notes* (Unknown Press 2014), *Bare Bulbs Swinging* (Artistically Declined Press 2013—winner of their Twin Antlers Poetry Prize), *Bound By Blue* (Sententia Books 2013), and a novel-in-stories, *Domestic Apparition* (San Francisco Bay Press 2011), which was also collected in *Three By Tuite* along with *Bound By Blue* and *Her Skin is a Costume* (Cowboy Jamboree 2023). She has also published five chapbooks of short fiction, flash, poetic prose, and multi-genre. She teaches online classes through *Bending Genres* and is an associate editor at *Narrative Magazine*. Her work has been published in over 700 literary magazines and over twenty anthologies including *Choose Wisely: 35 Women Up To No Good*. She has been nominated over 20 times for the Pushcart Prize, won first and second place in *Prick of the Spindle* contest, five-time finalist at *Glimmer Train*, finalist of the Gertrude Stein award and 3rd prize in the Bristol Short Story Contest. She is also the editor of eight anthologies. She is included in the *Best Small Fictions* of 2021, and Wigleaf's Top 50 stories of 2022, 2023. Her blog: MEGTUITE.COM.

About the Publisher

Whisk(e)y Tit is committed to restoring degradation and degeneracy to the literary arts. We work with authors who are unwilling to sacrifice intellectual rigor, unrelenting playfulness, and visual beauty in our literary pursuits, often leading to texts that would otherwise be abandoned in today's largely homogenized literary landscape. In a world governed by idiocy, our commitment to these principles is an act of civil service and civil disobedience alike.